Be Brave, Morgan!

Daredevil Morgan

Daredevil Morgan

by Ted Staunton

illustrated by Bill Slavin

rgan

Formac Publishing Company Limited
Halifax

Formac Publishing Company Limited recognizes the support of the Province of
Nova Scotia through the Department of Communities, Culture and Heritage.
We are pleased to work in partnership with the Province of Nova Scotia
to develop and promote our cultural resources for all Nova Scotians. We
acknowledge the support of the Canada Council for the Arts, which last year
invested $153 million to bring the arts to Canadians throughout the country.
This project has been made possible in part by the Government of Canada.

 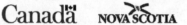

Cover design: Tyler Cleroux
Cover image: Bill Slavin

Library and Archives Canada Cataloguing in Publication

Staunton, Ted, 1956-, author
        Daredevil Morgan / Ted Staunton ; illustrated by Bill Slavin.

(Be brave, Morgan!)
Reprint. Originally published: Halifax, Formac Publishing
        Company, 2009.
ISBN 978-1-4595-0506-3 (hardcover)

        I. Slavin, Bill, illustrator   II. Title.   III. Series: Staunton,
Ted, 1956- . Be brave, Morgan!

PS8587.T334D37 2017   jC813'.54   C2017-905331-0

Published by: Distributed in Canada by: Distributed in the US by:
Formac Publishing   Formac Lorimer Books   Lerner Publisher Services
Company Limited   5502 Atlantic Street   1251 Washington Ave. N.
5502 Atlantic Street   Halifax, NS, Canada   Minneapolis, MN, USA
Halifax, Nova Scotia,   B3H 1G4   55401
Canada, B3H 1G4   www.lernerbooks.com
www.formac.ca

Printed and bound in Canada.

Manufactured by Friesens Corporation in Altona, Manitoba,
Canada in August 2017.

Job #236682

Contents

Chapter One

No Hands

My best friend Charlie and I are biking no-hands. Okay, Charlie is biking no-hands. I am biking both-hands because I wobble sometimes

which is scary.

Charlie says, "Know what the coolest ride is?"

"Wha' wun?" I am panting. Charlie is a fast pedaller, even no-hands. Going fast is okay, though. I want to get to my place and have snacks.

"The best ride is the GraviTwirl,"

says Charlie. "You stand against this wall and it spins

so fast you stick there, even when the floor drops away, and you can make yourself go upside-down."

"Coo-ool," I pant. "Let's go on it tomorrow." Tomorrow night is the Fall Fair. I love rides. I mean, I *will* love them. I have never been on a big ride before, but I don't tell Charlie because I can hardly wait to go on, so that is almost the same thing.

And I'm going to win a prize at the fair too.

Before I can pant all that,
we are at my place. Charlie
grabs his handlebars and pops
a wheelie. I don't. We take off
our helmets. I start to say "I'm
going to —" And that's when
we hear it:

scritch, scritch, scritch.

Oh-oh. I know that sound.
Sure enough, Aldeen Hummel
pushes around the corner on
her skateboard. Well, not on
her skateboard. Aldeen always
keeps one foot on the ground,

that's why you always hear
short scritches, never a long
scriiiiiiiiiiiitch.

"Hey," she yells, "you were
supposed to wait for me!"

Double oh-oh. I was supposed
to. Aldeen comes over to my
house after school when her
mom and her grandma are both
working. I hate that, because
Aldeen is the Godzilla of Grade
Three.

Now she scritches up

with her witchy hair bouncing.

She takes her foot off the skateboard. It keeps going without her and whams into the garage door. "Way to go," says Aldeen, pushing up her smudgy glasses.

"Let's eat."

We get snacks from my mom and go into the backyard. Charlie hangs upside-down from my play fort and tells us about the Octopus ride. I will say "Coo-ool" as soon as I finish chewing. Aldeen just says, "Your face is red." She's sitting on her skateboard.

Then she says, "Rides suck.

I'm going to win a prize in the
art contest."

Now is my chance. I swallow.

"I'm going to win a prize too.
Wait here."

I run into the garage.

"What is it?" asks Charlie,
climbing down.

"It's my pumpkin. I grew it
all summer at Grandpa's.

We just brought it home yesterday. It's for the Perfect Pumpkin contest at the fair."

I drag it out in my red wagon.

"Wow," says Charlie.

Wow is right. It *is* a perfect pumpkin. It's super round and orange, and it doesn't even have a scratch or a bump, and it's so big my dad could barely even lift it. It is also going to make the best Halloween jack-o'-lantern ever, after the fair.

Aldeen squints at it. "It looks like you," she says.

Huh?

She rolls over on her skateboard. "Is it heavy? Bet I can lift it."

Before I can stop her she jumps up and starts heaving.

"Aldeen," I say, "cut it out!"

GnnnnnnnnnnnUH!"

says Aldeen, still heaving.

15

Her teeth are clenched and her face is redder than Charlie's. "GnnnnnnnnnnnUH!" she says again, and rears. Her skateboard shoots out from under her foot.

"AHHHH!"

Aldeen goes flying back. The skateboard whacks my shin. I yell. Aldeen falls. My pumpkin drops. It lands on the patio with a big, fat *THWUNK*.

Then it isn't perfect
anymore.

Chapter Two

Less Than
Perfect

I am still mad when Aldeen's
grandma finally comes to get
her after dinner. Aldeen has
barely even said she's sorry.
First, she yelled, "Stupid
skateboard!"

Then she yelled, "I hurt my butt!" *Then* she yelled, "Stupid pumpkin!" while I hopped around holding my shin.

"You *wrecked* it," I yelled, still hopping.

All she said was, "Well, sor-reee. What'd you make it so heavy for?" Then she looked at my pumpkin. "You can just put some tape on it or something."

I could not just put some tape on it or something. There was a big crack right up the middle and a split in one side, too. My pumpkin is in a garbage

bag in the garage and I am
sitting at the kitchen table
being mad. My mom is in the
hall talking to Aldeen and
her grandma. I can hear her

grandma going, "Heh, heh, heh."

Aldeen's grandma is named Flo. She drives a taxi and she smokes little cigars. I like her, even if she does smell like cigars, but no way am I going out to say goodbye.

I am **so mad**, not even thinking about rides tomorrow can make me feel better.

The back door opens and my dad comes in with the pumpkin bag.

"Did you say goodbye to Aldeen?" he asks.

"No," I say. "All she wants
to talk about is how she's
going to win an art prize.

Dad puffs and puts the bag
down. Now his face is kind of
red too. He says, "Hey, kiddo,
it was an accident. You know

Aldeen didn't mean it. We're still going to have fun at the fair tomorrow. Think about all those rides."

Dad lifts the pumpkin out of the bag and puts it on the table. "And right now, you and I are going to do something with this."

"You can't just put tape on it or something," I say.

"Of course not," Dad says. "No sense letting a Perfect Pumpkin go to waste. We're going to make Perfect

Pumpkin **pies**."

Chapter Three

Expert Squisher

Dad says we are going to do it from scratch. He always says that, but **we never scratch anything.** He's a good baker. When we have cookies at our house, he makes them, and sometimes

I get to eat the extra cookie dough.

We get out the flour and the mixing bowl and the butter and the sifter and the rolling pin and the board and the measuring cup and the rattly silver pie plates.

"Get out the shortening please, Morgan," Dad calls. He's looking in the cupboard.

"We need salt too," I remember. "Excellent," says Dad.

I'm a good helper because I've done this before.

Dad measures and I mix in the big bowl with a wooden spoon and a fork. Then Dad spreads flour on the board and I get to flatten out the dough with the rolling pin. I love that part. It's like being a steamroller squishing everything. I go

"BLLLLLL- AAAP"

when I do it, like a rumbly
engine noise, and I pretend I'm
squishing Aldeen. It feels good.
Then I start thinking about all
the rides I'll go on tomorrow.
Charlie said there was one
called the Sizzler. We'll
have to go on that. And the
GraviTwirl and the Octopus one
too. Out in the hall, they are
still talking. I hear Aldeen say,
"Gra-a-a-an, let's go. I have to
do my picture."

Dad and I are fitting the
dough in the pie plates.

"Okay," Dad says, wiping up
flour.

"Now it's pumpkin time."

We put newspapers on the
kitchen table and put the
pumpkin on them. Then Dad
gets the big knife and starts
cutting chunks out of my
pumpkin. We reach into the
cold middle and start pulling
out seeds and stringy orange

pumpkin guts. My hands get super slimy in one second flat.

It is so gross, it's fantastic.

Pumpkin smell fills the kitchen. Dad scrapes off the chunks, then cuts them small and pops them into a saucepan to boil.

The blender is whirring when Mom finally comes into the kitchen. Dad has sugar and spices and eggs and milk out

on the counter. I'm squishing
pumpkin guts in both hands
to make the seeds come out.
We're going to save them. Mom
says something.

"What?" I say, when the blender stops.

"Pardon," says Mom.

"Pardon what?"

"No, *you're* supposed to say 'pardon' instead of 'what'," she reminds me.

Oh. Right. "Pardon?"

"Aldeen is coming to the fair with us tomorrow,"

Mom says, "until her Grandma Flo can meet us there after work."

"Wha-a-at?"

"It'll be fun," says Mom.

I squish harder.

Chapter Four

A Fair Start

So now it is Friday night and
we are going to the fair.
Everybody from school is
going. Last year we were
away when the fair was on,
and before that we didn't live
here. This time, though, it is

going to be so cool that I don't even care if Aldeen is with us. Charlie and I will go on about a

million rides

with everyone and too bad for Aldeen if she says that rides suck.

As we drive, Mom says from the front seat, "So, rides tonight and country fair things tomorrow: the farm animals, the —"

"Yeah, rides!" says Aldeen. She's bouncing as if she's on one already. Huh? I thought she —

"And games too!" she says.

"Maybe we'll win a prize,"

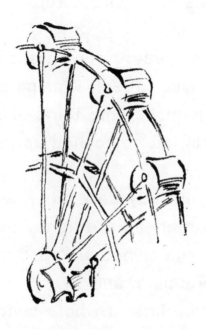

Dad says.

"And we have to go see
what prize my picture won,"
Aldeen says, bouncing some
more. "'Cause my mom took

it to the art contest this afternoon."

I look away. I don't want to hear about Aldeen winning a prize. It makes me think of my pumpkin, all smooshed up in pies.

It is already dark when we park. Up ahead are lights and music, and things are rattling and swooping, and every little while you hear a whole bunch of voices go

"wwwwWWWOOOAH!"

Even better, I think I can smell French fries.

There is a lineup at the gate.

We all get green wristbands.

Aldeen says, "Let's go see if my picture has won a prize yet."

"When your Grandma comes," says Mom. "She'll want to see too."

"Yeah," I say. "Let's go on rides." I am already looking for Charlie in the crowd.

It will be way more fun with him.

Mom and Dad buy tickets for us to go on five rides. The first ones we see are baby ones that go really, really slow.

Forget them. Then we pass the funhouse. Everything is

thumping and clanking, and music is blasting. A skeleton pops out and Aldeen jumps about twenty miles in the air and a monster laugh goes

"BWAH-HAHAHAHA!"

I only jump ten miles, so I laugh too — until Aldeen gives me her Queen-of-Mean look.

And then we're at the midway. It's crowded. Lights flash and this big rocket ride swoops and all the voices go "wwwwWWWOOOAH!" again. Then the rocket swings up, up, up, until it looks as if everyone is going to fall out of their seats.

Backwards.

Next to it another ride
has these little cage things
climbing up in the air and
tumbling upside-down, and over
there another one has all these
arms whooshing everybody in
and out so they scream and

twirl like crazy. I bet that's the Octopus. Just watching it makes my stomach go woozly.

Holy Cow. I swallow. I peek at Aldeen. Her mouth is open. The lights are flashing on her glasses. I look at the rides again.

Everything is so big. And fast. And loud. And swooshy.

I swallow again. It's all ... kind of ....

"Morgan! Morgan!"

I look and there's Charlie,

with Kaely and Mark and Paige,
lined up for a ride.

"Come on!"
Charlie waves me over.

I swallow one more time. "I
can't right now," I call back.
Aldeen is still staring. I point at
her, behind her back where she
can't see. "Soon."

Right now I'm almost
glad she's here.

Chapter Five

Bumper
Stars

"So," Dad says from behind me, "What do you want to go on first?"

The really, truly answer is — nothing. I didn't know the rides were going to be, well, **scary**. I don't say that, though.

I say, "Ummmmmm ...."

"How about the funhouse?"
Mom suggests.

"No way,"

says Aldeen, really fast.

Good. That skeleton was
kind of scary too.

"What, then?" says Mom.
"We have to use the tickets."

"That." Aldeen points.

Perfect: it's the bumper cars.
We hand in our tickets for the
next turn. This is going to be

good; I can hardly wait to bash into Aldeen a few million times.

Except I don't. The ride starts and

– BONK –

Aldeen rams into me from behind.

I try to turn and — BONK —
she hits me again. I spin the
wheel around and she zooms
off, then — BONK — gets me
from the other side.

The whole ride goes like
that until, finally, I have Aldeen
all lined up and

— ZOOP —

the power stops. The ride is over.

"That was cool," says
Aldeen. It was not. Then she

says, "I want to go see if my picture won a prize yet."

Before I can say no, Dad says, "Well, look who's here."

I'm hoping it's Aldeen's Grandma Flo, so she can take Aldeen away. But it's not. It's Charlie and the others, with their moms and dads. The grown-ups start talking. Charlie says, "We were just on the Octopus.

It was so coo-ool.

What have you been on?"

Just hearing "Octopus" makes my stomach go woozly again.

Kaely says, "We're going on the Orbiter next. Wanta come?"

"Which one is that?" I ask.

Kaely points. The Orbiter is little chairs like baby swings, way up in the air. They spin around this pole so fast that you lean sideways.

If anything breaks you'll fly off the fairgrounds into outer space.

My stomach goes even
woozlier. Oh, no.
What am I going
to do?

   Before I can
even think,
Aldeen says,
"That sucks.
Bumper cars."

   Behind her back I make
an awwwww face at Charlie.
I don't mean it, though.
Compared to outer space in a
baby swing, bumper cars sound
perfect.

Chapter Six

Bunny Hop

Really, bumper cars are even dumber than last time. Aldeen bashes me until I start to think that outer space in a baby swing might be fun after all.

"Now what?"Mom and Dad ask when we get off.

"Food!" I say. I can smell fries again.

"I want to see what prize my picture won!" says Aldeen, for the millionth time.

Dad says, "How about a game? You can use a ride ticket for one."

"But what about food?" I ask. Well, whine.

"If you're hungry, you should have finished your carrots at dinner," says Mom.

Geeeeeeez.

We pick a game where you throw darts at balloons. A sign

says everyone wins a prize and
I see just the one I want. It's a

giant gorilla

stuffed toy that will be
perfect for wrestling with and
snuggling into while I read or

watch TV. Wait till I show it to Charlie and everybody. They'll all want it like crazy. *And* I can say that I have to carry it so I can't go on any more rides. Perfect.

You get three throws. Aldeen goes first, and she is so crummy she only hits one balloon — and it doesn't even pop. Her prize is this furry little purple snake. How lame can you get?

Now it's my turn.

Whammo,
I break a balloon first time.

It's not the one I aimed at, but who cares? Everybody cheers. I throw again and the dart hits the board, but it bounces off and lands on a balloon and pops it. Everybody cheers again. Hey, am I good at this or what?

Now it's my last throw. I pick a balloon right in the middle. I scuff my feet. I stick my tongue between my teeth. I

take a big breath, lean back,
wind up — and Aldeen yells,

"GRAN!"

I jump. The dart flies out of
my hand.

"HEY!"

The man in the game dives
under the counter. The dart
lands right where his head
used to be. There is no balloon
there.

The man pops up from
behind the counter.

"Sorry," I say.

His eyes go all narrow. He
gives me a pink fuzzy bunny.

Oh, boy.

Chapter Seven

Chicken Talk

Aldeen does not even notice
she has wrecked my chance to
win a monster gorilla. She is too
busy blabbing like crazy to her
Grandma Flo, who is smoking
one of her little cigars and
trying to talk to Mom and Dad.

"Now we can go see my picture prize!"

Aldeen is tugging the sleeve of her grandma's leather jacket.

I look at her the way the man at the game looked at me. I do not want to go see Aldeen's stupid picture prize. If she had not yelled, I would

have won a monster gorilla
prize. If she had not dropped
my pumpkin, I would have a
Perfect Pumpkin prize too.

**Instead, what I have got is a
pink fuzzy bunny, and a sore
butt from getting bashed
around in bumper cars.**

And I don't have any French
fries either.

This stinks. If Aldeen wasn't
here, I would probably be
having a way better time. I bet
I would even be going on all
the rides, because it is Aldeen
who is more scared than me.

If I hadn't looked at her and
seen she was scared, I would
not have been scared.

No way would I have been scared with Charlie.

So it is all her fault. Once again, Aldeen has wrecked everything.

And now here comes Charlie and everybody back from

having fun on the Orbiter ride.
Charlie runs over to me.

"We have to go on that one
together," he says.

"It was awesome.

Hey, what's that?"

"Huh?" I say. "Oh, nothing. I
won it." I give the pink fuzzy
bunny to Mom. The grown-ups
are yakking again. Aldeen is
still tugging at her grandma.

"Is it ever cute," Paige says.

"I wanted a gorilla," I grump.
"Anyway, I can't go on any
more rides because now we
have to go see Aldeen's *art
prize*." I look, and Aldeen is

still busy with her grandma, so
I say, "And even if we didn't,
I still couldn't go because she
doesn't want to. She's chicken."

"I AM NOT."

Oh-oh. I turn. Aldeen has let
go of her grandma. Her eyes
are squinched. Her witchy hair
is zapping out from her head
and her noogie knuckles are

poking out from each fist.
Double oh-oh.

Then she says, "I'll go on anything you do."

I open my mouth to say "Yeah, right," and my voice has gone all squeaky. I sound like a fuzzy bunny. "What one?"

"That one." Aldeen doesn't even look where she points.

"Asteroid Belt?" says Charlie.

"Whatever," says Aldeen.

I swallow. It takes a long time. I squeak to Charlie, "Y-you coming?" I still sound like a fuzzy bunny.

The others shuffle a little. "I don't think so. We just got off the other one."

I get the tickets from Dad. He lifts his eyebrows, but he gives them to me.

We go join the lineup for the ride. Aldeen stares straight ahead. I watch the ride guy make sure everyone is tall enough to go on.

I bend my knees.

Aldeen glares at me and her noogie knuckle pops out again.

I stand up straight.

The ride guy lets us by. A seat stops in front of us. We get on. Another guy fastens us in. We don't talk. There's a hum and a jolt, and the ride is on.

Chapter Eight

Asteroid Belted

I scream for every second of the whole ride.

It lasts about two days — at least it feels as if it does. I can't tell you much else about it, because I keep my eyes shut

after the first time we drop, dan-
gle face-down, and then rocket
up backwards. All I can do
is hang on as hard as I can
to whatever I grab and keep
screaming, even after my lips
get smooshed together and my
knees come out my nose.

I am still screaming when
I finally feel everything slow
down, but a tiny "Eeeeeeeee"
is all I have left. I can't
hear me because someone
else is still screaming too
—"EEEEEEEEE" — but I can feel
my scream in my teeth. They
are clamped shut, but vibrating.
Something hurts too.

I sneak one eye open. Whew, we are right side up, close to the ground. I look around. Aldeen still has her eyes shut tight. She is the one who's still screaming too.

The ride stops. So does she. She looks at me. I look at her.

"Ow," we both say.

Now we can see what hurts too. We are squished together in the centre of the seat, holding on to each other so tight our fingers have gone all white.

Chapter Nine

Keeping Your Beak Shut

Aldeen and I are almost in each other's laps. One of my hands is clamped onto Aldeen's arm. The other one won't let go of the safety bar in front of me. My own arm feels as if Aldeen has squeezed right through it.

Slowly, we get untangled. My face feels hot; Aldeen's is all red.

We scooch over to our own sides.

We don't say anything and we don't look at each other.

Luckily, our car stopped at the back of the ride.

When it's our turn to get off, everybody is waiting at the bottom of the steps and they are all talking at once.

"How was it?" asks Kaely.

"Yeah,"' Mark calls. "Was it good?"

My legs are all wobbly.
I think I can talk now without
barfing but I don't know what
to say.

**I can't say, *I was so
scared I shut my eyes the
whole time and held on to
Aldeen and screamed,***

because I'll sound chicken.
And I can't lie and say, *I liked
it* but Aldeen was so scared
she shut her eyes the whole
time and held on to me and
screamed because then she
will say I did too and probably
pound me. And for sure I can't

say, *We were so scared we shut our eyes the whole time and held on to each other and screamed*, because that makes us both sound chicken — and even worse, smoochy — and Aldeen will probably double pound me.

Which means all I can do is ... is ...

is ...

I look at her. She looks back at me. Her mouth is pinched tight. I can't tell if she's mad or if she feels sick.

I say, "It was ... really wild."

I look at Aldeen again. She still doesn't say anything, so I say, "But cool, though. It was cool."

"Was it scary?" Paige asks.

"Well ..."

Before I can think of something, Aldeen shrugs and says, "A little, but no biggie. For a ride, it didn't stink."

Her voice sounds kind of cracked but nobody notices.

Instead, "Coo-ool," they say.
"Let's go on!"

"Where's the line?"

"Hey," I say to Charlie.
"Didn't you already go on that one?"

"No way," says Charlie.

"Nobody ever goes on Asteroid Belt.

It's the scariest one here.
You're the first one to do it.
You going to come on again?"

"Not right now," I say. "We have to check out Aldeen's picture."

"Not my picture," she says.
"My prize."

Chapter Ten

Perfect
Prizes

All the prize stuff is in a big
building at the end of the
midway. Mom is still carrying
my bunny from the game.
Guys who go on Asteroid Belt
don't carry pink fuzzy bunnies.
I wonder if Aldeen has really

won a prize for her picture.
Aldeen does do pretty good
pictures. I was over at her
house once and saw a bunch of
them pinned up in her room.

The building is a hockey rink
with no ice. It is full of things
people have entered in the fair
for prizes. There is no time
to look at any of it because
Aldeen zooms us along to find
her picture in the art show.

Before we even get there,
she's yelling
"TOLD YOU! I WON! I WON!"

Up ahead, one of the pictures has a red ribbon stuck on the corner. When we get up close, I see it's a picture of a guy with this big jack-o'-lantern in a red wagon, only the guy is almost as round as the pumpkin and his face is kind of like the jack-o'-lantern one. The title says *Perfect Pumpkin* by *Aldeen Hummel*.

"Morgan," my mom smiles,

"I think that's you!"

What? No way.

But Aldeen says, "Yeah. You can have it. I just want the ribbon."

She starts to rip the picture down, but Grandma Flo says,

"Aldy, you have to wait till the fair is over."

I look some more at the picture. **That's me?**

My face gets hot again.

"Hey," Dad says. "While we're here, let's look at some other things."

So we do. Most of them are boring, like jars of jam, and knitting, and lawn chairs with happy faces woven into them. Some of them have ribbons on, too. There is one table with

nothing but little plates of seeds on it. Why would you get a ribbon for seeds, I wonder. I like the weird vegetables, though.

There is a carrot that looks like a zombie,

with arms and legs, and a bunch of potatoes that look like people's heads. The winner is a cucumber like a snake.

Then I see the table with the pumpkins. I point. "Is that where we would have brought my pumpkin?" I ask Dad.

"Yup," he says.

I look at the pumpkins. At first, they look pretty perfect. Then I look closer. The huge one with the red ribbon is lopsided. The super-round one with the blue ribbon is too little. The white ribbon one has a flat bit. The others all have lumps and bumps somewhere; scratches or scuff marks.

Not one of them is as perfect as mine was.

Behind me, Aldeen is saying "But I want my ribbon now."

"Ixnay on that," says Grandma Flo. "This way the whole world gets to see what a great picture you did."

I sigh. Nobody is going to see what a great pumpkin I grew.

Dad says, "Say, look over here."

Oh yessss. There are tables full of cakes and cookies and pies. I start to feel a little better.

"Hey," Mom calls, "Check out this one."

BEST
FATHER/SON
BAKING

It's a pie. A pumpkin pie. The red ribbon is on the card with it. The card says *Best Father/ Son Baking*, then there is my name and Dad's. It's one of our pies.

"They turned out so well I thought we should enter one," says Dad.

"Looks like your pumpkin won a prize after all."

I stare. Then I say, "Hey, there's a piece missing."

"They have to taste it to

decide," Dad explains.

"I haven't even tasted it. Can we have some now? I'm hungry."

"No," says Mom, "We have to leave it so everyone can see what a good job you did. Let's share some fries instead."

"And how about another ride?" asks Grandma Flo.

"There are enough tickets for one more," Dad says.

I know what's coming:

"Bumper cars,"

says Aldeen.

It sounds good to me.

Morgan the Brave

Morgan has to figure out how to go to a birthday party— but avoid seeing the scary movie promised as the main event. Birthday boy Curtis tries to expose anyone missing out on his party as a chicken, so Morgan needs an idea, and quick! Is it possible that Aldeen, Morgan's frenemy who never fails to notice and taunt him about his weaknesses, has the solution? Morgan finds that not everyone is as tough as they look.

Morgan on Ice

Be Brave,
Morgan!

Morgan on Ice

Ted Staunton / Illustrated by Bill Slavin

Morgan doesn't like to skate, and he's deter-
mined not to learn. What he really wants to do
is go see Monster Truck-A-Rama with Charlie.
Aldeen is not impressed since Morgan already
agreed to go to Princesses on Ice with her. Can
Morgan keep everyone happy, or is he skating
on thin ice?

Morgan's Got Game

Morgan is left out of the loop when everyone at school begins bringing their Robogamer Z7 to school, linking up online with one another, and playing at recess and lunch. Charlie lets Morgan use his Z7 every now and then, but clearly you're not cool unless you have one of your own.

Poor Morgan is reduced to playing other games with Aldeen for something to do. Finally his parents relent, but Morgan learns that sometimes gaming is more trouble than it's worth!